For Herb
C. R.

For Peter
D. G.

When I was a little girl, I lived with my grandparents in the country. Our house was small and white. It had an old coal stove to keep us warm and a tiny little kitchen for supper and a nice back porch for the dogs.

In the summer I sat in our swing
and ate fresh tomatoes and sang.
In fall I helped can apples. In spring
I took long walks with my granny.

And in winter,
I waited for Christmas.

Winter in the country is so quiet.

The snow slows everything down.

Birds are silent and serious.

Dogs stay in their warm houses.

Children want cocoa and blankets.

Everyone is ready
for something really special.

Everyone is ready

for Christmas.

My grandfather always got our Christmas
tree from the woods behind the house.
Off he'd go with his ax while my
grandmother and I pulled boxes of
old ornaments from her closet, which
smelled like wool and mothballs.

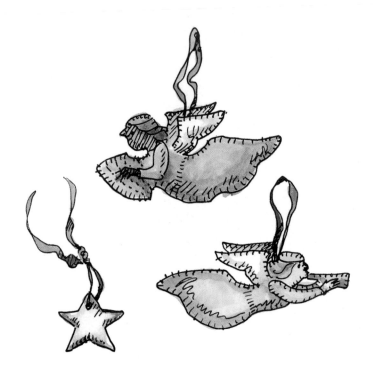

I loved those ornaments. Some of them I
had made myself. Hard foam bells glued
with green glitter. Red construction-paper
chains. There were silver icicles and
white glass stars and soft angels. Each
ornament reminded me of my whole life.

Grandfather always brought home a tree
that was a little too wide or a little too tall and
we would have to spend the next few weeks
squeezing around it in the living room. It seemed
sometimes like an embarrassed guest. But
we loved that tree and couldn't wait to turn on the
lights at night. It was the prettiest thing we had.

On Christmas Eve my grandparents and I went to services at the small Baptist church at the bottom of the hill. I got to stand up front with the other children and sing a Christmas carol for the grown-ups.

Afterward, each child was given a small brown bag full of candy and nuts and a tangerine. I gave my grandfather the tangerine because I knew he loved them.

My grandparents and I walked home
from church through the snow and into
our warm little kitchen. We pulled off our
wet boots and gloves and hung them near
the stove to dry. Then my grandmother
helped me write a note to Santa Claus
while my grandfather rested.

I left Santa a saucer of cookies and
a glass of milk and the nicest note
I could think of. Then I went to bed.

And in the morning when I woke it was
still a little dark outside and still a little
shivery, and I went to my grandparents'
bed and asked them to help me see
what Santa brought. And they rose up
from their warm quilts and together
we all went to the tree.

Every Christmas Santa gave me just
what I wanted: a new doll. And he
always gave me something else I hadn't
asked for and which was a surprise.
A paint-by-number kit. A bear bank.
A coloring book. His cookies were
always gone, his milk glass empty.
I was glad Santa liked everything.

I went to church again with my grandparents, later that Christmas morning. They let me take my doll. The service was short because the preacher knew everyone wanted to play with their toys and bake their hams.

He just reminded us what Christmas
was about and sent us home.

And all that day there were aunts and
uncles and cousins knocking at the door,
neighbors dropping off pies, and dogs
barking at all the commotion
and waiting for leftovers.

My grandparents and I kept our Christmas
tree for as long as we could, and then
finally, after the New Year, it was time
to take it down. Grandfather hauled it
out to the woods while my grandmother
and I put the ornaments away. We swept
up the needles and tinsel. Then we
all had milk and a biscuit.

Christmas in the country was over.
There were spring walks and
summer tomatoes and fall apples
to look forward to now.

But in that closet of wool and
mothballs, there would be boxes
of old ornaments, waiting.